Acting Edition

The Winter Guard Play

by Avery Deutsch

‖SAMUEL FRENCH‖

No one shall make any changes in this title(s) for the purpose of production. No part of this book may be reproduced, stored in a retrieval system, scanned, uploaded, or transmitted in any form, by any means, now known or yet to be invented, including mechanical, electronic, digital, photocopying, recording, videotaping, or otherwise, without the prior written permission of the publisher. No one shall share this title(s), or any part of this title(s), through any social media or file hosting websites.

For all inquiries regarding motion picture, television, online/digital and other media rights, please contact Concord Theatricals Corp.

MUSIC AND THIRD-PARTY MATERIALS USE NOTE

Licensees are solely responsible for obtaining formal written permission from copyright owners to use copyrighted music and/or other copyrighted third-party materials (e.g. artworks, logos) in the performance of this play and are strongly cautioned to do so. If no such permission is obtained by the licensee, then the licensee must use only original music and materials that the licensee owns and controls. Licensees are solely responsible and liable for clearances of all third-party copyrighted materials, including without limitation music, and shall indemnify the copyright owners of the play(s) and their licensing agent, Concord Theatricals Corp., against any costs, expenses, losses and liabilities arising from the use of such copyrighted third-party materials by licensees. For music, please contact the appropriate music licensing authority in your territory for the rights to any incidental music.

IMPORTANT BILLING AND CREDIT REQUIREMENTS

If you have obtained performance rights to this title, please refer to your licensing agreement for important billing and credit requirements.

THE WINTER GUARD PLAY was first produced by Southeast Missouri State University in March of 2023. The performance was directed by Kennneth L. Stilson, with set design by Amber Marisa Cook, costume design by Emma Whetton, lighting design by Chris Haug, sound design by Hankyu Lee, and choreography by Dr. Trudy C. Glasi. The stage manager was Kyra Ankrom. The cast was as follows:

CAROLINE . . . . .Kinya Kairigi
JESS . . . . Ally Wukitsch
LUCY . . . . Lizzie White
LIZ . . . . .Cecilia Hartney
MAYA . . . . Isabel Kissel
MINDY . . . . Jodie Lloyd
ZOE . . . . .Anne Roach
UNDERSTUDIES . . . . Elise Bowles, Evie Rodenbaugh, Paris Heaver

CHARACTERS

CAROLINE – A senior: Hates conflict. Good cop. Best friends with Jess.

JESS – A senior: Feels more like a jock than a theatre kid. Bad cop. Best friends with Caroline.

LUCY – A junior: Never dropped a single flag. Driven AF. Extremely direct.

LIZ – A junior: Does she only talk to her flag? Gifted.

MAYA – A junior: Pretending to be sixty-five. VERY smart. Raises her hand a lot.

MINDY – A sophomore: New to the team. Wants to be liked.

ZOE – A sophomore: New to the team. Young Bernie bro. "Rad."

SETTING

The entire play should take place in some version of a high school gym. At the end of the play, there is a giant tarp with the Earth on it stretched across the stage.

AUTHOR'S NOTES

Everyone in this play is trying to make a good routine. There are some people who are more outspoken than others, but no one is trying to be cruel. And when they are cruel, it costs them something.

The Titles: The titles of each scene (which are bolded and in ALL CAPS) are announced over loudspeaker by the same announcer who introduces the dances.

Winter Guard: Winter Guard is explained within the play further – but for background, it is a kind of competitive lyrical dance routine using flags and sabers usually performed in a giant stadium. It's born out of Color Guard, but most definitely its own very epic thing. Routines I have seen have wrestled with human trafficking, eating disorders, and our dependency on foreign oil.

In an ideal world, a pre-show with Winter Guard videos playing on loop (projected somewhere, or on a tv screen or playing in the lobby) would set the tone nicely.* The energy in the theater should be that of a sports arena.

The combination that inspired this play is Mechanicsburg High School's 2014 combination titled "Forever Young." It can be found on YouTube.

---

* A license to produce *The Winter Guard Play* does not include a license to publicly display any third-party or copyrighted images. Licensees must acquire rights for any copyrighted images or create their own.

DEDICATION

Thank you to Silvia Bond, Emma Maltby, Julian Socha, Angelica Santiago, Amber Avant, Ashley Hildreth, Ella Escobar, Reagan Stovenour, Laura Lee Caudill and Kayla Peters for inspiring these characters and believing in this play (and my writing) before I did. And to Emily Moler, without whom this play would not exist.

PROLOGUE

*(House lights are up. Seven teens walk onstage. Six get into child's pose. One [**MAYA**] walks downstage and plugs her phone into a speaker. She presses her phone. Music starts from a speaker onstage.* She pauses it.)*

MAYA. Nothing's happening.

JESS. *(Still in child's pose.)* Did you press the /

MAYA. Yes.

CAROLINE. *(Still in child's pose.)* Try the /

LUCY. Just say it Maya

JESS. *(Getting up.)* Wait

> *(**JESS** goes to help **MAYA**. The rest of the group stays in child's pose, but some are now looking up, resting their head on their hands etc.)*

LUCY. *(From child's pose.)* We have

JESS. Hold on.

LUCY. We only have

ZOE. One day we knowwww

LUCY. It's tomorrow I'm saying it's / tomorrow

ZOE. We get it we dude we /

JESS. Just give me a /

LUCY. *(Impersonating a booming announcer's voice.)* PERFORMING THEIR PROGRAM /

CAROLINE. Lucy!

LUCY. THE LAST EARTH DAY MID-ATLANTIC INDOOR NETWORK IS PROUD TO PRESENT MECHANICSFIELD HIGH SCHOOL.

(The music starts to play again.)

JESS. *(Yelling over the music.)* You guys start I'm just gonna keep /

LUCY. My earth.

*(As **THE TEAM** rolls up their spines, **LIZ** moves to the center and does a very impressive lyrical dance.)*

JESS. *(From her spot downstage.)* My planet.

MAYA. *(Running back to the circle.)* My oceans.

CAROLINE. My mountains.

MINDY. My sky.

MAYA. My air.

ZOE. Clear.

JESS. Blue.

ZOE. Green.

MAYA. Beautiful.

CAROLINE. Beautiful.

ZOE. Beautiful.

LUCY. Sinking.

JESS. *(From her spot downstage.)* My city.

LUCY. Sinking.

CAROLINE. My town.

LUCY. Drowning.

MAYA. My forest.

LUCY. Burning.

CAROLINE. My creatures.

LUCY. Dying.

MINDY. Floods.

MAYA. Flooding me.

LIZ. Flooding you.

CAROLINE. My earth.

MAYA. My earth.

LIZ. My earth.

THE TEAM. *(Unison.)* Look what you did to me.

ANNOUNCER. *(Coming out of the onstage speaker.)* PERFORMING THEIR PROGRAM THE LAST EARTH DAY / MID-ATLANTIC INDOOR NETWORK IS PROUD TO PRESENT MECHANICSFIELD HIGH SCHOOL.

JESS. Got it!

LUCY. Well now we have to start over.

> *(Blackout.)*

ANNOUNCER. *(Now being heard throughout the house.)* Eight weeks earlier!

> *(Spotlight on **MINDY**.)*

MINDY PRAYS BEFORE HER FIRST PRACTICE

MINDY. Hi God! It's me. Mindy.

How are you?

I'm good. I'm doing good.

I'm doing – oh my god sorry – thank you!!! Being new – sorry! – Moving to a new school is so much better – so much easier – now that I made the team and you for sure helped me with that so yeah thank you definitely thank you – sorry! Sorry for not starting with that.

…

I'm gonna ask for another thing but you totally don't have to do it.

Like.

No pressure.

I was just hoping

I mean it's not a big deal but I was just hoping

I was hoping maybe you could make me into an entirely different person than like I've ever been before??

Because I don't know

The past few years everyone's been saying "you're so brave" and it was like. Nice. But also confusing? Because I…that wasn't really how it felt. To me.

I mean. You know how I felt. Obviously.

…

Do you remember the new tall diving board? In elementary school?

We talked about it back then but um

Basically it was really high. And the fall was um. Really far. And all the other kids did it.

First thing. And I sorta had to sit back and watch for a while?

I don't wanna do that today.

I don't wanna sit back.

I wanna be the type of person who does dive in. Right from the start.

I wanna be the type of person who does that.

Yeah.

So if you could make me the type of person who can do that – I'd really appreciate it.

But if you don't want to

That's okay.

Seriously!

You've already done so much.

WEEK 1: THE PRESENTATIONS

*(Lights up. **JESS** stands. **LUCY** is stationed next to the dry erase board with a marker. The rest of **THE TEAM** is seated. The board reads as such:)*

(Lucy: World War One Revisited.)

(Maya: Dodd Frank you Lied to me!)

(Caroline: "Manifest" Destiny's Child.)

JESS. So it's about gun control.

LUCY. Oooooh very cool

JESS. Because like let's turn this gun play on its head ya know? Like sure it's fun watching us throw these rifles but like what if they were loaded? Like how twisted is it that all of us have been playing with weapons like five times a week since we were eight? I mean it's kind of insane.

ZOE. Yes!! Hold that mirror UP!

MAYA. Guys I'm sorry.

LUCY. MAYAAA

MAYA. I'm sorry!

JESS. Maya come on.

MAYA. Are we sure we don't wanna call her?

LUCY. And beg?

JESS. No thank you.

MINDY. Maybe there's someone we could ask in town?

LUCY. No one in this town knows anything about Winter Guard.

CAROLINE. Yeah she sorta brought Winter Guard here.

MINDY. Really? A lot of people knew about Winter Guard in Fort Collins.

JESS. Coach was a bitch – we're better off without her.

LUCY. Today is presentation day.

MAYA. Lucy.

LUCY. We should be focusing on the presentations.

MINDY. Why did Coach quit?

JESS. Because she's deranged.

MAYA. She had a delicate /

JESS. Delicate??

MAYA. Delicate temperament. But without her we wouldn't even know Winter Guard exists we wouldn't /

LIZ. *(To her flag?)* We didn't win with a coach...

CAROLINE. What Liz?

JESS. She's saying we didn't win with a coach – which is true!

LUCY. We are wasting time!!

MAYA. Lucy it's one day.

LUCY. We have exactly *sixty days* to put together our routine and if we do NOT start presentations today – we will have exactly *fifty-nine days* to put together our routine.

MAYA. But /

LUCY. You know what's the difference between a gold medalist and a silver medalist??

MINDY. Good luck?

LIZ. *(To her flag.)* Type of metal.

LUCY. One. Day.

MAYA. Lucy! Teams need leadership they need /

JESS. Caroline and I will lead the team. We're the seniors.

MAYA. Respectfully. That might not work.

JESS. Respectfully. I think it will. Right Caroline?

CAROLINE. Um…

MAYA. I think we should call her…

JESS. Right Caroline?

ZOE. Sorry sorry are we talking about doing this totally sans adults?

MINDY. Right yeah are we doing this um without any grown-ups?

> *(Ugh. Did* **MINDY** *just say grown-ups?)*

LUCY. Does that scare you?

ZOE. HECK NO. Sign me up REVOLUTION BA-BYYYY

MINDY. Haha

Yeah!

Revolution!

> **(MINDY** *has never said that word before.)*

JESS. Caroline? Are you kidding me?

CAROLINE. Sorry. No. I mean yes!! No one's calling Coach – okay?

JESS. No one.

CAROLINE. She went too far last year. Right?

JESS. Right.

LUCY. Can I just say. I saw her drop a flag once

CAROLINE. And if she's not down with us then we aren't down with her you know what I mean?

JESS. Yep.

LUCY. Her grip was sloppy. Her grip was undeniably sloppy.

MAYA. But /

JESS. Maya. It's me or her.

MAYA. ...

CAROLINE. It's gonna be good Maya. Trust us.

MAYA. Fine.

Fine.

LUCY. THANK YOU

JESS. So back to my idea? Guns?

ZOE. So important. So so so so important.

MINDY. Um...my dad owns a gun?

LIZ. *(Is she talking to her flag?)* Mine too.

CAROLINE. Um I feel like Jess is talking less about um... owning guns and more about loving guns?

JESS. Yes It's not anti-gun – although I am anti-gun – but for the combination it would be like –

ZOE. It's like anti-worshipping at the *feet* of the gun!

JESS. Yes.

Sure.

Okay.

ZOE. *(Nodding, proud of herself.)* That's totally what it is.

> **(LUCY** *writes "Jess: Anti-worshipping at the feet of the gun.")*

CAROLINE. Uhh alright Mindy!

MINDY. *(Startled.)* What??

CAROLINE. Take it away!

MINDY. Oh right. Wow. We just like zipped through those first ones!

Haha!

…

Okay!!!

Here's what I'm thinking:

"An Ode to Moms"

"Seven Teens Say Thank You"

LUCY. *(Sarcastic.)* Awesome.

JESS. Lucy. Respect the presentation.

> (**LUCY** *glares. Does a gesture of "wiping the moment off her shoulders."* **THE TEAM** *mimics her gesture in unison.* **MINDY** *and* **ZOE** *don't know it.)*

MINDY. What did you just do?

CAROLINE. It's our forgiveness gesture

JESS. Keep going Mindy

MINDY. Oh

Cool

So uh okay.

We would all be versions of our parents getting ready in front of the mirror.

Like in old-timey clothing or whatever.

And then the mirrors are actually made of flags. Like the flags are embedded in the mirrors.

Somehow.

I think it's possible.

I don't know – I just moved here last year but I saw the healthcare show and it was amazingggg.

(**CAROLINE** *gives* **MINDY** *an encouraging nod.*)

Right!

So then I guess we like

We would reach out and take the flags and the mirrors would fall down.

And all of a sudden

There would be like water

Like a pond or something.

Like very Greek.

Very

(Says it wrong.) Narcississus.

MAYA. *(Says it right but is nice about it.)* Narcissus.

MINDY. *(Doesn't hear the difference.)* Uh huh!

And then we would reach into the mirror like we were reaching into ourselves.

And then we would all look out at the audience and say: "Thank you Mom!"

CAROLINE. That's really sweet!

LIZ. *(To her flag?)* Not everyone has Moms.

JESS. *(Looks at* **LUCY**.*)* Oh.

MINDY. What?

JESS. I didn't think before /

LUCY. It's fine. Forget it

MAYA. *(Raises hand.)* What if they all said "Thank you parents!"

MINDY. Ummm...sure? Sure. Parents work too! I'm sorry, did I /

LUCY. I'm good. K?

> (**LUCY** *wipes the moment off her shoulders.* **THE TEAM** *mimics again.* **MINDY** *deflates.*)

> (**LUCY** *writes "Mindy: An Ode to Parents!"*)

CAROLINE. K. Who's next? Zoe?

ZOE. Cool cool cool amazing okay one sec let me get my props one sec.

> (**ZOE** *runs offstage and comes back on with multiple props. A soccer ball, a burlap sack, and a vision board that she has covered with a sheet. She positions herself as if preparing to give a TED Talk.*)

Okay. I have a question for all of you. What do you think is the biggest problem facing young people globally?

MAYA. Stagnant wages!

CAROLINE. Social Media!

LIZ. *(To her flag?)* Everything.

ZOE. Ooh really good ones. I'm thinking about something else though. Anything else seem like a big problem for like the world's young people? I'm talking children.

MINDY. Global warming?

> (*Pause. Genius.*)

CAROLINE. Oh my god. I love that.

JESS. Mindy, that's killer.

ZOE. Yes. Wow. Global warming is an awesome idea.

LUCY. That would score fucking high on Nuance.

JESS. Wait yeah they'd all think it was like some super G-rated Earth Day bullshit. And then we'd be like ummmm NO the Earth is dying people. You two are geniuses!!

CAROLINE. Yessssss sophomores get ittttt!!

JESS. AWESOME presentation Zoe and Mindy.

ZOE. Oh wait wait wait wait wait. Sorry that's awesome Mindy. Love it. But actually sorry I just sorta had a different idea that I think would also be amazing.

> (**ZOE** *pulls the sheet off the vision board.*)
>
> (*It is covered with horrifying images of child labor.*)

Child labor. Because okay yes I know that we don't personally work as child laborers because we live in Pennsylvania but if we want to make a combination that's about the world at large – not just American kids – then child labor should be front and center. Or global warming – I mean that is also definitely a widespread issue.

MINDY. No but child labor is really good too.

> (*As* **ZOE** *delivers this monologue she is increasingly overwhelmed by her own genius.*)

ZOE. Thanks! Okay okay so wait I'll just lay it all out. We could be like on an assembly line in the beginning. Like this. Like we are all lined up. And we are manufacturing our rifles and flags and sabers. So like we're making them at first. And we could wear like really tattered clothes and like have dirt on our faces and stuff. And I was thinking it could be to the soundtrack of *Mudbound*. Which wasn't about child labor but was like a very important movie.

ZOE. Anyway so we're all in unison. And I was thinking throughout the song in the beginning section we could have voice-over statistics about child labor. Like one of us could record it, and my brother has a really nice GarageBand setup so we could totally do it at my house.

And the tarp I am imagining could be like a map of the world, and it could show all the places in the world where there is child labor and like then there could be arrows showing how all those goods go to the U.S. And – this is jumping forward sort of – but the like underlying theme of the combination would be like "AUDIENCE! YOU ARE COMPLICIT!!!!"

And we could be doing really sad lyrical dancing for like the first minute, but no actual tricks. So the audience will be like "The fuck?!?! We came here for Winter Guard!"

(*Very professional.*) This idea is awesome because we would definitely be playing with their expectations so it's not only, like socially responsible, but also theatrically super exciting.

Because okay after that first minute, the music would change to like an epic symphony.

Like something really bombastic and explosive. Like I imagine the sensation being like if the walls legit exploded and everything bad in the world like crumbled down and out of all that rubble something way better is born. Like a Harry Potter Phoenix situation.

And then we would all look up at the audience and be FREE. Like really free. And we would throw all of our guns up in the air and our flags and our sabers and we would all catch them in unison, and then we would do an insane combination. Like we would break out of the line and it would be in unison still but like a super joyous unison. And then these wings, that we actually had all along would sprout out of our backs and it would be like – what would happen if everyone who was being taken advantage of, what if they just said – "Fuck you bitches for taking my life and my body I'm a fucking bird and I'm gonna fly away and run the world and leave you leeches to rot."

And then we would all grab hands and scream over and over and over:

I'm FREE

I'm FREE

I'm FREE

I'm FREE

I'm FREE

I'm FREEEEEEEEEEEEEEEEEEE!!!!!!!!

> *(Loooooooooong beat.)*

MAYA. *(Raises her hand politely.)* I think global warming is better.

CAROLINE. Your idea is awesome Zoe.

JESS. It's awesome.

CAROLINE. I got goosies.

LUCY. Maya's right. I mean guys. The Earth is dying.

JESS. That's true. It is like literally dying.

ZOE. No no I hear that.

CAROLINE. Even though child labor is important!

MAYA. *(Raises her hand again.)* I just think global warming is more time sensitive. Example! By the time we graduate college, there might not be a Florida.

LUCY. Would that be bad?

JESS. Lol.

MINDY. Wait. Sorry. I love Florida?

CAROLINE. Should we vote on it?

LUCY. No, we have to do global warming. I mean we can't not. Everything else is irrelevant if the Earth is dead.

MAYA. Agreed.

ZOE. Heard. Heard.

CAROLINE. Maybe we could incorporate child labor – like do an industrial revolution flashback sequence or something??

ZOE. That could be cool! Okay. I'm in. Let's do global warming.

MINDY. Are you sure global warming isn't too um. Intense?

LUCY. The more intense the better.

ZOE. Totally! Love that!

JESS. So it's decided.

LIZ. *(Sort of to the group, sort of to her flag.)* We should vote.

JESS. I mean...

LUCY. I think everyone is decided

LIZ. *(Again, sort of to the group, sort of to her flag.)* If this is a democracy we should vote.

> *(Beat.)*

MAYA. Let's vote!

> *(Beat.)*

JESS. Everyone close your eyes.

> *(Everyone but **LUCY** closes their eyes.)*

MINDY. *(With eyes closed.)* If all of our eyes are closed, who counts?

LUCY. I count. Because I've been on the team since I was a freshman and I'm good at keeping secrets. Everyone keep your eyes closed and don't peek. I'll see.

All in favor of global warming?

(Everyone but **MINDY** *raises their hands.)*

The ayes have it. Let's save the Earth bitches.

(Blackout.)

R.I.P. TO REJECTED ROUTINES

(A large tarp with a skull and crossbones is spread across the stage.)

ANNOUNCER.   Performing their program, "R.I.P. TO REJECTED ROUTINES" Mid-Atlantic Indoor Network is proud to present Mechanicsfield High School.

(The teens roll up their spines as they did at the start of the play.)

LUCY. World War One Revisited

CAROLINE. Manifest Destiny's Child

MAYA. Dodd Frank You Lied to Me

JESS. Anti-Worshipping at The Feet Of the Gun

MINDY. An Ode to Parents

ZOE. Child Labor

(A song in the style of "My Heart Will Go On" begins to play. Something epic and timeless about love and loss and devotion.)*

*(****THE TEAM*** does a lyrical routine in honor of the fallen presentations. Each flag says one of the rejected routines. They dance with the flags and then fold them delicately on*

---

* A license to produce *The Winter Guard Play* does not include a performance license for "My Heart Will Go On" by Celine Dion. The publisher and author suggest that the licensee contact ASCAP or BMI to ascertain the music publisher and contact such music publisher to license or acquire permission for performance of the song. If a license or permission is unattainable for "My Heart Will Go On," the licensee may not use the song in *The Winter Guard Play* but should create an original composition in a similar style or use a similar song in the public domain. For further information, please see the Music and Third-Party Materials Use Note on page iii.

the ground as if they are folding a flag atop a casket. At the end of the dance **THE TEAM** *stands in a line and does the "wipe your shoulders off" gesture. Everyone exits except for* **LUCY** *and* **MAYA.**)

WHAT ABOUT COACH?

*(**LUCY** and **MAYA** wait to be picked up.)*

MAYA. Who's gonna choreograph? Who's gonna buy the tarp? Who's gonna run face rehearsal?

LUCY. Are you forty-five?

MAYA. What?

LUCY. You act like you're middle aged.

MAYA. No I don't...

LUCY. It's gonna be better. Now we can make all the decisions.

MAYA. Lucy this is gonna be like a group project on steroids.

LUCY. I like group projects.

MAYA. That's because I always do the work for you!!

LUCY. Wow your eyes just got so big.

MAYA. And at States they are definitely going to notice and /

LUCY. Maya! Do. Not. Take this from me.

MAYA. ...

Do you think Jess meant it today? When she said it's me or her?

LUCY. I don't know. I don't really think about Jess.

MAYA. What do you think about?

LUCY. Winning.

(A horn honks.)

My dad's here.

Can you send me the Latin notes?

MAYA. Sure.

*(**LUCY** leaves. **MAYA** is left alone on stage.)*

(Spotlight.)

SMALL TALK

MAYA. Sometimes when I'm doing Winter Guard I like to count every person in the audience who doesn't want to be there. I count them while I avoid watching the other teams, so I don't get in my head. There are usually way more people who don't want to be there than people who do. Upwards of 65–76%. And then I pick one person, and I watch them the whole time. And then when I go out on the floor, I say in my head: "change their mind" – and then I do multiplication tables in my head – but I do them like a prayer. I can't really explain it, because I'm not praying in words, but it's like I'm sending the math to them. Math is really spiritual for me. I like that God made something that makes sense. And I send the sense to them. Like if I get every answer right, they'll know. And then in my body it feels like I'm praying too. And the whole combination becomes this big swirl of math, and tempo and counting and praying and flags – and it's like this big gust of wind and it's all wrapped up inside of me and it's pushing me to that one person I picked who doesn't want to be there. And when the number is over I look up, and I find their face. And I scream right at them. Right at their face. It's weird – but that's my favorite way to talk to people.

(Blackout.)

WEEK 2: THE SHARING CIRCLE

(Everyone is sitting in a circle. All their eyes are closed, except for **MINDY**.*)*

CAROLINE. Dead polar bears.

LUCY. Sweltering heat. Like the kinda heat where everything sticks to you.

JESS. New York City underwater.

MAYA. Food shortages.

CAROLINE. *The Walking Dead.*

ZOE. Zombies.

JESS. Power outages.

CAROLINE. Darkness.

MAYA. Carbon pollution.

JESS. Cars.

LUCY. Canned goods.

CAROLINE. Dead seals.

MAYA. Hurricane Sandy.

CAROLINE. Dead dogs.

MAYA. Hurricane Irene.

MINDY. *(Confused.)* My Aunt Irene?

JESS. Exxon Mobil.

CAROLINE. Dead frogs /

MINDY. What are we doing?

(Everyone opens their eyes.)

JESS. We're vision boarding.

MINDY. What?

LUCY. Vision. Boarding.

JESS. Have you never done this?

LUCY. Why did you sit there for that long if you didn't know what we were doing?

MAYA. Did you say Aunt Irene?

MINDY. Was that wrong?

ZOE. I didn't really know either. I was just sorta free associating.

CAROLINE. You said good stuff though! Zombies was good!!

LUCY. We vision board. Before we choreograph a piece. We free associate. So that it's personal.

CAROLINE. Coach's whole approach was about making things personal. She always would say why do *you* need to tell this story

JESS. It's basically the only good thing she taught us.

MAYA. That's why she started the team.

LUCY. So we could make some art that actually hit home.

CAROLINE. Not just some canned Color Guard BS.

JESS. Literally fuck Color Guard.

MINDY. We don't like Color Guard?

(*They all look at* **MINDY**. *Beat.*)

LIZ. (*For once making eye contact.*) Color Guard is the enemy.

CAROLINE. Nothing is worse than Color Guard.

JESS. Even global warming.

LUCY. Literally.

CAROLINE. Mindy, this is super important to understand.

JESS. Winter Guard is a completely different animal. Like a different species.

JESS. Like a way more evolved species.

MAYA. Color Guard doesn't have thumbs

LUCY. That's why none of us do it.

MINDY. But. Didn't you guys do it in middle school?

JESS. Everyone does things in middle school they regret.

LIZ. *(Filled with meaning.)* Everyone.

CAROLINE. Don't beat yourself up! We all started there.

MINDY. I really liked Color Guard back home though.

(Again **THE TEAM** *stares.)*

JESS. You don't like Color Guard.

LUCY. You just think you do.

MAYA. Stockholm Syndrome.

CAROLINE. Mindy. It's important to say goodbye to Color Guard.

JESS. There's a reason none of us do Color Guard.

LUCY. Because it's dangerous.

MAYA. It creates very bad habits.

CAROLINE. Coach's number one rule was "don't do Color Guard"

JESS. Her only good rule.

MAYA. Winter Guard is much better.

LUCY. And harder.

CAROLINE. People don't get it, but Winter Guard is a completely different art form. It's SO messed up that it's not in the Olympics.

JESS. Criminal.

MAYA.   Last year I had to leave Thanksgiving early for practice and my grandparents were like "Maya can't you take one day off from cheerleading??" and I had to go downstairs and scream into our second freezer.

JESS. Disgusting.

LUCY. And a lot of teams are pay to play now.

MAYA. So wrong.

LUCY. You have to pay thousands of dollars to be on a team.

MAYA. Because the art form is so egregiously undervalued.

CAROLINE. And none of the colleges I'm applying for have teams.

JESS. Me neither.

LUCY. College teams are expensive too!

MAYA. So unethical.

JESS. Color Guard is like "lalalalalala I'm having fun it's a football game look at me I can throw flags like twice in unison. Yay I love sports hahaha wow look at me do tricks like a dog."

LUCY. Winter Guard is like, "Hello I'm a fucking ninja I'm going to throw fourteen flags perfectly in unison and they will all land right on time, and oh wait this whole dance isn't about the football team winning it's about the importance of democracy or the accessibility of health insurance in America."

MINDY. That was an amazing routine.

CAROLINE. My grandma still talks about the pre-existing conditions dream sequence.

ZOE. But you didn't go here last year?

MINDY. Huh?

ZOE. How'd you see their routine you didn't go here last year?

MINDY. Um. Yeah no I lived here for a little while before starting school.

MAYA. The scoring system alone /

LUCY. The scoring system of Winter Guard is the most dynamic scoring system in modern American sports.

ZOE. Seriously????

JESS. They use these fucking INSANE descriptors.

CAROLINE. You're scored on Nuance, Adherence to Equipment, Stamina, Recovery, Detail.

ZOE. Sick!!

MAYA. And each section is out of ten. And each number range has a descriptor. It's SO cool.

> (**MAYA** *begins drawing this on the dry erase board.*)

JESS. 1–20's called "rarely discovers." Like you rarely discovered Detail, or you rarely discovered Adherence to Equipment.

LUCY. Then 20–40 is "sometimes knows." Like sometimes you know about Stamina.

CAROLINE. And then 40–60 is "frequently understands." Like, usually, you understand Nuance – but then once in a while – you don't.

MAYA. And then 70–90 is "always applies." Like you always know about Nuance or Recovery or Stamina

ZOE. What's 90–100?

> (*Everyone sighs.*)

LUCY. "New standards."

MINDY. What's that mean?

MAYA. It means that there is a score in Winter Guard that if achieved, means you have done better than previously believed POSSIBLE.

ZOE. So like, there's a score that basically means you're the best in Winter Guard history?

LUCY. YES.

JESS. Last year we got 80s on four out of five sections.

LUCY. We got an 88 on Nuance.

MAYA. But we've never set new standards.

CAROLINE. That's why global warming could be the silver bullet. We could definitely get a 100 on Nuance.

JESS. And after this year, us seniors will never get to do it again.

MAYA. And people who do curling can keep doing it in college.

JESS. Unreal.

CAROLINE. Mindy. Zoe. Are you ready to say goodbye to Color Guard?

LUCY. You can never go back.

MAYA. But it's sooooooo worth it!

LUCY. Repeat after us.

CAROLINE. *(Getting excited.)* We do this every year!!

JESS. Everyone

> *(The whole **TEAM** gathers in front of **MINDY** and **ZOE**.)*

THE TEAM. Goodbye Color Guard

MINDY & ZOE. Goodbye Color Guard

THE TEAM. Goodbye football games

MINDY & ZOE. Goodbye football games

THE TEAM. You served us well

MINDY & ZOE. You served us well

THE TEAM. Now go to hell!

MINDY & ZOE. Now go to hell!

THE TEAM. Hello Winter Guard!

MINDY & ZOE. Hello Winter Guard!

THE TEAM. The most sacred of sports.

MINDY & ZOE. The most sacred of sports.

THE TEAM. Color Guard is to Winter Guard

MINDY & ZOE. Color Guard is to Winter Guard

THE TEAM. As pants are to shorts.

MINDY & ZOE. As pants are to shorts.

THE TEAM. I will toss my flag

MINDY & ZOE. I will toss my flag

THE TEAM. And catch it every time.

MINDY & ZOE. And catch it every time.

THE TEAM. I will tell a story

MINDY & ZOE. I will tell a story

THE TEAM. That is distinctly mine.

MINDY & ZOE. That is distinctly mine.

THE TEAM. Winter Guard. Winter Guard. Winter Guard for life.

MINDY & ZOE. Winter Guard. Winter Guard. Winter Guard for life.

EVERYONE. *(**MINDY** and **ZOE** join slowly but by the end they are in perfect unison.)* Winter Guard for life. Winter Guard for life.

For life. For life. For life. For life.

FOR LIFE FOR LIFE FOR LIFE FOR LIFE FOR LIFE FOR LIFE FOR LIFE.

(Blackout.)

FACES PART 1

(**THE TEAM** *lines up downstage.* **ZOE** *is in the audience.*)

ZOE. Confusion!

(**THE TEAM** *makes a face of confusion.*)

Anger!

(**THE TEAM** *makes angry facial expressions.*)

Evil!

(**THE TEAM** *makes evil faces.*)

Am I doing good?

MAYA. So good!

MINDY. Haha this is hard...

CAROLINE. It's so important though. Our whole bodies have to tell a story. Even our faces.

MINDY. Right. Yes. My whole body.

ZOE. Afraid!!

(*Blackout.*)

LIZ AND HER FLAG HAVE A WALTZ

(Lights up. The stage is empty. **LIZ** *walks into the gymnasium. No one is there. Except her flag. She looks around. Makes sure she's alone. Picks up flag. Holds it close. She closes her eyes. She's been waiting all day for this. She starts to sway back and forth. A gentle rock. Starts to hum. Something faint. Music comes in.* Very old Hollywood. The two waltz.)*

(Blackout.)

---

* A license to produce *The Winter Guard Play* does not include a performance license for any third-party or copyrighted music. Licensees should create an original composition or use music in the public domain. For further information, please see the Music and Third-Party Materials Use Note on page iii.

IS GLOBAL WARMING MINDY'S FAULT?

   (MAYA, LIZ, MINDY, ZOE *and* **LUCY** *sit onstage. Stretching.)*

ZOE. Dude. It's a BIG deal.

MINDY. It's not.

ZOE. No dude it IS.

MINDY. I just said it by accident.

MAYA. And we loved it!!!

LUCY. And you're a first year.

ZOE. Big deal dudeeee.

MINDY. Do you think we'll win?

MAYA. Depends on our work ethic.

LUCY. Oh we'll fucking win.

MAYA. Depends on our team-unity.

MINDY. Do you think the judges will like global warming?

MAYA. Depends on the judges unfortunately.

ZOE. Who won last year?

MAYA & LUCY. Farming

MINDY. What?

MAYA. Last year Fox Lane /

LUCY. The high school that won

MAYA. Did their show about farming.

LUCY. No fucking principles.

LIZ. *(To her flag?)* Great art is not about farming.

MAYA. Liz it's not about the content it's about the execution. I mean think about Van Gogh. With the wheat.

LIZ. *(To her flag for sure.)* Do you want to be in art about wheat?

MINDY. *(To* **ZOE**.*)* Who is she talking to?

   *(***ZOE*** shrugs.)*

MAYA. But yes Liz is correct. To quote my Father, "Their combination was not worth a hill of beans."

LUCY. It was so dumb they like had all these tractors. It was total spectacle.

MAYA. They got a 98 on Adherence to Equipment. Just because of the tractors.

LUCY. Last year was garbage on so many levels.

ZOE. That was when Coach yelled at Jess?

MINDY. Wait what happened?

ZOE. Jess dropped her flagggg

MAYA. She *almost* dropped her flag

MINDY. Wait what?

ZOE. Dude. You know about this.

MINDY. No I don't?

ZOE. Dude. You do.

MINDY. No I really don't! I never hear gossip, no one ever tells me gossip.

MAYA. Jess almost dropped her flag last year.

   And then Caroline caught it.

LUCY. But we still lost points.

MAYA. And then Coach yelled at Jess.

LUCY. And then Jess yelled at Coach.

MAYA. Which Coach didn't like.

LUCY. Surprise, surprise.

MAYA. So she quit.

LIZ. *(To her flag.)* Good riddance.

MAYA. And now our team is run by seventeen-year-olds.

LUCY. Which is cool, Maya. Normal people think that's cool.

MAYA. I don't think either of us are experts on what normal people think Lucy.

ZOE. That's sort of childish right? Like quitting just 'cause someone yelled at you.

MAYA. Coach had a very delicate ego.

LUCY. She was a bitch.

MAYA. As my mom would say /

LUCY. Is a bitch.

MAYA. "She's a yeller."

LUCY. Although I don't know maybe she's dead.

MAYA. Lucy! She's not dead.

LUCY. I dunno – Winter Guard was her whole life.

MAYA. She started the team.

LUCY. She was a prodigy in Ohio.

MAYA. Her house was all trophies, very garish.

LUCY. But I saw her drop a flag once.

MAYA. Lucy, we know.

MINDY. Do you guys ever see her? Around town?

ZOE. That would be soooo awkward.

LUCY. If I saw her I would walk the other way.

LIZ. Same.

LUCY. Whatever, she's irrelevant now.

MINDY. Do you really think we can win??

LUCY. I bet Fox Lane does their combination about like National Parks this year. Fucking cowards

ZOE. Hate that. It's like say something ya know?

MINDY. Like, global warming isn't too "out there" right?

MAYA. Define "out there" Mindy?

ZOE. I wanna do something super controversial. That's just my taste.

MINDY. I mean... I just hope it was a good idea. I hope I didn't like ruin the team or anything

(**JESS** *and* **CAROLINE** *enter.*)

JESS. Let's get started people!

(*Blackout.*)

FACES PART 2

(The entire team is lined up downstage. Except for **JESS** *who is seated in the audience.)*

JESS. DESPAIR!

> *(***THE TEAM*** makes faces that communicate despair.)*

BLOODLUST!

> *(***THE TEAM*** makes faces that communicate bloodlust.)*

HOPE!

> *(***THE TEAM*** makes faces that communicate hope.)*

JOY!

DESPAIR!

JOY!

HOPE!

BLOODLUST!

JOY! BLOODLUST!

LUSTIER!

LUSTIER!

Okay. Stop.

Caroline. You seem distracted.

CAROLINE. What?

JESS. Are you thinking about something else?

CAROLINE. No. I'm thinking about Bloodlust.

MAYA. It can help to picture someone you actually are bloodlusty towards.

LUCY. Yeah, picture an enemy.

CAROLINE. Um. I don't really have any enemies.

JESS. ...Lucky you.

Okay let's try again.

DESPAIR

(Blackout.)

*(***THE TEAM*** leaves except for **CAROLINE**, who pulls out her phone.)*

CAROLINE LEAVES A MESSAGE

(**CAROLINE** *is on her phone on the other side of the gym.* **JESS** *enters but* **CAROLINE** *can't see her.*)

CAROLINE. So then we did the sharing circle which went well but I was wondering if you had any ideas about the best way to /

JESS. Who are you talking to?

CAROLINE. Ah! Oh my god. You scared me.

JESS. Who are you talking to?

CAROLINE. No one. I mean. I was just talking to my grandma.

JESS. About Winter Guard?

CAROLINE. Well. She's a big fan. Of our work.

(*Beat.*)

JESS. Did you get my text?

CAROLINE. Yeah. Um. Honestly, I think you should be Dance Captain.

JESS. Why?

CAROLINE. I mean. You're a way better leader than me.

JESS. But you're a way better dancer than me.

CAROLINE. That's not true.

JESS. Jesus Caroline

CAROLINE. What?

JESS. Everyone wants you to be Dance Captain.

CAROLINE. I don't even know if people would vote for me.

JESS. Everyone will vote for you.

CAROLINE. And if we lose it'll be my fault.

JESS. We're not gonna lose. We're gonna fucking win.

CAROLINE. Well okay but /

JESS. Caroline.

Come on.

It's our senior year. Do this with me.

CAROLINE. Right.

Okay.

Yes.

Yes. Of course yes.

I want that.

WEEK 3: CAROLINE IS ELECTED DANCE CAPTAIN

(The dry erase board is out.)

*(It reads: Jess: General Manager, Maya: Tarp Master, Liz: Keeper of the flags. Everyone sits with their eyes closed. Except for **LUCY**.)*

LUCY. All in favor of Zoe as Audio Liaison?

(Everyone raises their hands.)

ZOE. *(Her eyes closed, hand raised.)* I could have like another job like um. Like Art Director or /

LUCY. No this is your job. All in favor of Caroline being Dance Captain.

*(Everyone but **LUCY** raises their hand. She takes a second to contemplate throwing the election. She had hoped to be Dance Captain. But then **MINDY** opens her eyes. **LUCY** immediately raises her hand.)*

The ayes have it! Obviously!

*(**CAROLINE** squeals.)*

*(Spotlight on **LUCY**.)*

LUCY CATCHES FLAGS

LUCY. I've never not caught a flag. Not at a tournament. Not at a practice. Never.

People don't believe me when I say that. And I understand why. Because it's an insanely amazing gift, and people don't believe that other people have gifts unless they see it in front of them with their own eyes. That's a very sad part about human nature. But I don't judge it because if someone told me they never dropped a flag I would say "Wow! That's amazing!" and then I would turn around and pretend to choke on my own vomit because liars make me wanna throw up.

But I'm not lying.

My dad is scared about what I'd do if I ever dropped a flag. He says I'm "projecting onto the flags." I told him, "I have no idea what the fuck that means" but I was lying.

Obviously I know what that means. I'm sixteen I know what projecting means. But I told him that, because I don't want to stop.

I competed one week after my mom died. I caught every single flag.

That's why I don't really hang out with people who don't do Winter Guard. They don't get that nothing on Earth – is better than catching a flag – falling from fourteen feet in the air – right when you're supposed to.

And that's the thing about humans. When they see bliss that they can't have – they'll try to take it.

    (Blackout.)

WEEK 4: WHEN DOES THE BLEEDING START?

(Lights up. **THE TEAM** *is in a complicated pose – the circle from the start has fallen to the ground and they are splayed out, in strange sculptural shapes. They speak from these weird shapes.)*

JESS. And after we rip off the flower crowns – that's when Lucy will start bleeding.

CAROLINE. I thought we decided Lucy would bleed after she throws the flag with the carbon-emission statistics?

MAYA. We have audio for that right?

JESS. Yeah Zoe's brother is doing it with GarageBand right?

ZOE. Totally. My brother is like a total audio genius.

CAROLINE. Hold on I need to look at this from the outside

*(***CAROLINE*** leaves the weird shape.)*

JESS. But back to the bleeding /

LUCY. As long as I'm bleeding within the first forty seconds. Those first forty are everything.

MINDY. Where are we gonna be bleeding from?

ZOE. I mean she should be bleeding from her hands right?? Like symbolically??

MINDY. What?

ZOE. Like, there's blood on her hands dude.

MINDY. Global warming isn't all Lucy's fault!!!

LUCY. We can't bleed from our hands.

CAROLINE. Why?

LUCY. Uh. 'Cause we have to catch flags?

CAROLINE. Right. Right right right.

JESS. So where does she bleed from?

LIZ. *(To her flag, chuckling.)* Her eyeballs.

MAYA. Perhaps her head?

LUCY. How do you suggest we do that?

MAYA. A wide-rimmed hat??

JESS. That sounds messy

CAROLINE. Maybe like her arms? Or like her shoulders? From this angle her shoulder would look good.

LUCY. Why would I bleed from my shoulders?

ZOE. Dude blood comes from anywhere. Like our whole bodies have blood.

MINDY. Can we get out of these poses?

CAROLINE. Sorry yeah everyone relax.

(The group relaxes.)

MAYA. It's gonna be hard to make decisions like this without an adult.

MINDY. Yeah a grown-up right now would be nice!

LUCY. Don't say grown-up.

MINDY. Sorry.

CAROLINE. Guys I think we should just stay on task

JESS. Thank you. Yes.

LUCY. We are wasting timeeeeee.

JESS. What's our decision on the blood?

(Silence.)

CAROLINE. Maybe we can sleep on it?

JESS. Fine. Everyone go home and journal and tomorrow we vote.

>(**THE TEAM** *gets up and scatters.* **JESS** *goes to* **MAYA**.*)*

Maya?

MAYA. Yeah?

JESS. Did you order the tarp?

MAYA. Uh huh

JESS. The one with the big Earth on it?

MAYA. Mhm. And my parents said we don't even need to pay them back.

JESS. Oh shit. That's really nice.

MAYA. And they bought us pre-show outfits?

JESS. Oh.

MAYA. In like our school colors.

JESS. Well that's…nice.

MAYA. They love supporting the arts.

JESS. Right. Well. See you tomorrow.

MAYA. Jess?

JESS. Yeah?

MAYA. Are you okay? Like about last year? Because if you ever wanted to talk about /

JESS. About how you blame me for Coach quitting?

MAYA. I didn't say that I /

JESS. Or how you blame me for us losing?

MAYA. I don't blame you I /

JESS. It's cool, I'm kidding.

MAYA. What?

JESS. I'm joking around. I seriously think it's funny.

MAYA. Think what is funny?

JESS. What happened last year it's honestly funny. Being humiliated in front of the whole team and then absolutely no one having my back. I think it's really fucking funny. And I love when people bring it up.

MAYA. ...

JESS. See ya.

> (**JESS** *exits.* **MAYA** *stands alone onstage. Anxious.*)

WEEK 5: THE FIRST FORTY

(**MAYA** *is alone, center stage.*)

(Gershwin-esque music swells as the teens rush on, encircling **MAYA**.* *Half the group carry blue flags and dance frantically. The other half have silk ribbons. They do a manic ribbon dance. The flags get more and more chaotic. And then wait? Somehow* **LUCY***'s ended up in the middle and she's drowning. She's drowning. And then blood starts to gush out of her mouth. And a flag goes into the air.* **LUCY** *reaches for it. Something happens. She turns around. The flag isn't caught.)*

LUCY. Ow!

CAROLINE. HOLD!

LUCY. You stepped on me!

MAYA. Lucy. You dropped your flag.

LUCY. It's not my fault!! Someone stepped on me!!!!

JESS. *(A challenge.)* Who did?

LUCY. *(Thinking on her feet.)* Mindy! She stepped on me.

MINDY. No I didn't!!

LUCY. You fucking stepped on me. I'm bleeding.

CAROLINE. Well…yes?

LUCY. Not from my mouth! From my foot!!

MINDY. I didn't do it I swear!!!

---

* A license to produce *The Winter Guard Play* does not include a performance license for any third-party or copyrighted music. Licensees should create an original composition or use music in the public domain. For further information, please see the Music and Third-Party Materials Use Note on page iii.

JESS. Zoe! Did Mindy step on Lucy?

ZOE. Umm...

JESS. You were right there. Did she step on her?

ZOE. Hey no, I can't speak to that I didn't get a visual.

MINDY. Lucy, I swear on my dead dog it was not me.

LUCY. *(Freaking out.)* Well SOMEONE stepped on me 'cause I wouldn't have dropped it /

MAYA. Lucy, are you okay?

JESS. Let it go Lucy.

LUCY. Are you kidding?

JESS. No. Chill out.

> *(Stand-off. A hot second.* **LUCY** *does the wiping off her shoulders.* **THE TEAM** *mimics.)*

Care. Wanna lead reflections?

CAROLINE. *(Getting the hint.)* Yes. Great. Reflections. How did that feel for everyone?

LUCY. I'm a mess.

CAROLINE. Do you want less blood?

LUCY. I don't wanna be sticky the whole show.

JESS. Maybe we could research less sticky blood...

ZOE. Um can I just say something separate from the sticky factor?

JESS. Uh. Sure.

ZOE. I feel like there should be more blood.

MINDY. What!?!

CAROLINE. Why?

ZOE. Just like. Realistically. If the world ended there would be more blood.

JESS. Do we have research on that?

MAYA. It hasn't happened yet. So...no.

ZOE. It's just a little too pretty right now. I mean. To me. It looks kinda tame with just Lucy bleeding.

LUCY. You want us all to bleed?

MINDY. That's very messy

LUCY. I don't think we need all seven of us to be drenched in blood.

MINDY. Then everyone will be sticky!!!

ZOE. We don't have to be drenched. I just feel like if only you are bleeding it looks like it's a piece about just you bleeding to death.

CAROLINE. I think we need to zoom out for a sec.

JESS. Yeah, agreed.

CAROLINE. What do we want the audience to feel? Like what's the goal for us?

ZOE. Complicit.

MAYA. Motivated

JESS. Revelation.

LUCY. Guilty

LIZ. *(To the flag? Is this an inside joke between the two?)* Like they have to pee

CAROLINE. Okay. Okay.

> **(CAROLINE** *writes all these thoughts down.)*

So I'm gonna like summarize these themes...

It seems like we want to be scary, but look good doing it.

JESS. Literally put that on my tombstone.

CAROLINE. So. Here's the thing. As long as the choreo is awesome and the flag shit is on point, we're gonna look sweet. So the question is how scary do we wanna look.

(Beat. **THE TEAM** *considers.)*

MAYA. I think we should do full blood.

JESS. What?

MINDY. Really Maya????? Really??

MAYA. Zoe's made good points.

ZOE. HECK YES I DID!

MINDY. Maya slow down slow down we don't need to do this.

CAROLINE. Lay out your reasoning

MAYA. Well I'm just thinking about our three audiences. Judges. A bunch of grown-ups. And the other teams. The more visceral the higher our score.

ZOE. Yep.

MAYA. The more depressing the worse the adults will feel.

ZOE. CORRECT.

MAYA. And the more hardcore, the more intimidated the other teams will be.

ZOE. BINGO!

MAYA. And generally, intimidated competitors choke.

ZOE. Micro and macro – *this* plan checks out.

CAROLINE. Mindy do you wanna articulate your concerns?

MAYA. *(Excited.)* Should we get the debate gavel?

JESS. No, I think we can keep this casual.

MINDY. I guess I just... I don't know, I feel weird like um... Making my parents feel bad?

LUCY. Well that's sort of the whole point of the show.

MINDY. But um my family really looks forward to seeing me in things and /

ZOE. Mindy JOIN US on the blood side. I promise there's room for you *and* your family here.

LIZ. *(To her flag.)* And the tarp should bleed too.

CAROLINE. What Liz?

LIZ. The tarp should bleed too.

JESS. Is that even possible?

ZOE. My brother's friend Dylan is super good with art and stuff – He could paint us a second tarp!!

MINDY. Are we really sure we want to do this? I mean. It's gonna be so crazy. It just seems. I don't know, it just seems like really crazy.

LIZ. *(To her flag.)* We don't want to leave here with any regrets.

> (**CAROLINE** *and* **JESS** *exchange looks.* **CAROLINE** *nods.)*

JESS. Let's do it.

> *(Blackout.)*

LIZ AND HER FLAG DO A VICTORY SAMBA

(Lights up. **LIZ** *walks onstage. No one else is there. She finds her flag on the ground. She dramatically dips it, very* Dancing with the Stars. *A sexy song comes on.* [*] **LIZ** *and her flag Samba. It's hot.)*

(Blackout.)

---

[*] A license to produce *The Winter Guard Play* does not include a performance license for any third-party or copyrighted music. Licensees should create an original composition or use music in the public domain. For further information, please see the Music and Third-Party Materials Use Note on page iii

MAYA TRIES TO CHECK IN

(**MAYA** *and* **LUCY** *stand in their coats, waiting to be picked up.*)

MAYA. Lucy, it's not a big deal. We all know you wouldn't have dropped it.

LUCY. It's fine.

MAYA. It wasn't your fault. It was Jess she /

LUCY. I shouldn't get distracted so easily.

MAYA. You've never dropped a flag.

LUCY. Well not anymore. Now Liz holds that title.

MAYA. If you want this weekend we could practice together? We could go to the park my dad would drive us and /

LUCY. I was surprised you were pro-blood

MAYA. Yes… I was surprised as well.

LUCY. I think you're right though.

MAYA. Logically, if the Earth becomes uninhabitable there will be a lot of blood.

LUCY. Yep

MAYA. It's kind of scary to think about.

LUCY. What is?

MAYA. Everyone on Earth…bleeding that much…

LUCY. Yeah

…

Can I copy your trig take-home?

WHO STEPPED ON LUCY?

(**CAROLINE** *and* **JESS** *wait to be picked up.*
JESS *is on her phone.*)

JESS. *(Googling.)* All fake blood is sticky.

CAROLINE. Why did you step on Lucy?

JESS. I don't know why did she blame Mindy??

CAROLINE. Uh

JESS. I didn't do it on purpose! It's just like. It's not the biggest deal in the world dropping a fucking flag.

CAROLINE. Totally.

JESS. Like I'm just over these juniors losing their shit every ten minutes.

CAROLINE. Right.

JESS. Did I tell you Maya's weird lawyer parents bought us warm up outfits?

CAROLINE. Seriously?

JESS. It's like, we get it Maya, your parents are rich.

CAROLINE. At least the sophomores are cute?

JESS. Yeah I feel bad Lucy blamed Mindy.

CAROLINE. That was really sad when she swore on her dead dog...

JESS. I'm just like tired of everyone being such whiny bitches.

CAROLINE. *(Joking.)* Hello Coach!!

JESS. *(Hurt.)* Are you serious?

CAROLINE. No I'm kidding! Come on.

JESS. K.

> *(Beat.* **CAROLINE** *takes out her phone.* **JESS** *rolls her eyes.)*

Calling your grandma again?

CAROLINE. What?

JESS. Nothing.

IS ALL THIS BLEEDING MINDY'S FAULT?

> (**ZOE** and **MINDY** *wear coats and wait to be picked up on the other side of the stage. Mindy's coat is extremely puffy.*)

MINDY. It's cool you have an older brother. Who like, drives you places.

ZOE. Yeah it's nice. Nice to not have to ask my mom.

MINDY. So jealous.

ZOE. He thinks the theme is super dope.

MINDY. Really?

ZOE. Yeah. He loved it.

MINDY. Wow that's cool. I've sort of been nervous about /

ZOE. Wait. Do you have siblings?

MINDY. Yeah. One of five. I'm the oldest.

ZOE. Oh that's cool. 'Cause like you always get to ride in the front seat and stuff.

MINDY. Yeah. That part's cool.

ZOE. It's weird I didn't know that!

MINDY. What?

ZOE. It's weird I didn't know you had siblings. I'm used to knowing everything about everyone.

MINDY. Yeah.

ZOE. Everyone I know has lived here forever.

MINDY. Sure.

ZOE. Do you miss – where are you from?

MINDY. Colorado?

ZOE. Yeah do you miss it?

MINDY. Not really.

ZOE. That's cool. You're like. "I'm open to new shit, universe."

MINDY. Um. Yeah. I guess.

ZOE. That's very mature.

MINDY. Thanks.

ZOE. Wait so when did you move here?

MINDY. Um. Two years ago?

ZOE. But you didn't start school until this year?

MINDY. Yeah I was um. Sorta sick?

ZOE. Shit. I didn't know that.

MINDY. I'm better now so it's fine.

ZOE. So you moved here…to get better?

MINDY. My grandparents are here so it was. They could watch my brothers when I was um. Getting better.

ZOE. Wow.

MINDY. I'm totally good now though so. It's like all fine.

(Changing the subject.) Your brother is like. Really good at soccer.

ZOE. Yeah. He's Mechanicsfield famous.

MINDY. I mean there aren't that many guys on the soccer team and in band ya know?

ZOE. That's true.

MINDY. His girlfriend seems nice.

ZOE. They broke up.

MINDY. *(This is great news.)* Oh. Why?

ZOE. I don't know. I feel like she dumped him. 'Cause he's like very mopey around the house right now.

MINDY. *(Trying to conceal her joy.)* Wow. That's sad. I thought they were cute.

ZOE. Yeah. I don't know. I feel like she wasn't on his level. Like spiritually ya know?

MINDY. *(She doesn't know.)* Oh yeah. Totally.

ZOE. He like meditates and stuff.

MINDY. Wow. SO cool

... ...

He's gonna come to States right?

ZOE. Oh for sure. My parents legit don't even know what Winter Guard is but he's like really into it.

MINDY. My parents keep calling it cheerleading.

ZOE. So offensive.

MINDY. Yeah... But hey that's cool that your brother is coming. That's really cool. Then we really gotta be good haha right? This whole global warming thing – it's gotta go well right?

ZOE. Haha yeah. I guess.

MINDY. Just between us – I really wish we weren't doing this whole bleeding thing I really wish we were /

ZOE. Oh he's here. See you tomorrow!

  (**ZOE** *runs off.*)

MINDY. Yeah. Yeah. See you!

  (**MINDY** *sits alone for a moment. Blackout.*)

WEEK 6: DO THE ICE CAPS NEED A NIGHT OUT?

> *(***CAROLINE***,* ***ZOE***,* and ***MAYA*** *are doing a sequence of choreography. The sequence is to a song in the style of "Ice Ice Baby."* * *The rest of* **THE TEAM** *is watching.* **CAROLINE** *holds.)*

CAROLINE. And this is when we would hand out the donation buckets for the NRDC /

LUCY. What is this song?

MINDY. Who are they again?

CAROLINE. Plus there's gonna be fog.

LIZ. *(To her flag.)* Musical legends.

MINDY. No no the letters?

MAYA. *(Her version of gossiping.)* The National Resource Defense Counsel. Very reputable place, my mother does probono work there and LOVES the higher-ups.

JESS. Where are we getting fog from again?

CAROLINE. Zoe.

ZOE. Yep yep yep my brother's friend Crystal from Starbucks runs a haunted house and she said we can totally borrow it

MINDY. Isn't it a little like...forward? To make people give money?

LUCY. People don't have to give money. It's like at church. They don't have to donate anything, but then they have to be stingy in front of all their friends.

---

* A license to produce *The Winter Guard Play* does not include a performance license for any third-party or copyrighted music. Licensees should create an original composition or use music in the public domain. For further information, please see the Music and Third-Party Materials Use Note on page iii.

MAYA. Shame is a powerful motivator there's no denying it.

ZOE. That would be so dope. If we like won *and* raised like six thousand dollars for the planet. I mean. We'd be on the NEWS probably. Not that I care about that.

CAROLINE. Rewind does anyone have any questions about the dance?

LUCY. So this is about the ice caps melting?

CAROLINE. *(Really excited.)* Yeah, I call this sequence – the "Ice Caps' Last Night."

ZOE. So cool. It's like the ice caps are at the club, before the world ends.

JESS. That's funny. To imagine ice caps like drunk.

MAYA. *(Teasing/sucking up.)* Jess you are bad!!

        (**JESS** *is confused but smiles?*)

MINDY. This looks hard

CAROLINE. It's not. It's not that hard. Right guys?

MAYA. Very teachable.

MINDY. It looks really hard to me.

ZOE. You'll totally get it dude!

LUCY. What are we going to do about the blood?

CAROLINE. During the dance?

JESS. Cocoa power instead of corn syrup

CAROLINE. Huge difference. We tested it. Huge, huge difference.

LUCY. So it's chanting, then drowning, then bleeding, then hip hop dance, then volcano then rage then dead?

ZOE. Yep.

LUCY. Sick.

MINDY. Um I was thinking what if we raged and then um didn't die?

JESS. No it's better if we die.

LUCY. Definitely.

CAROLINE. And there'll be flag stuff too!!

LUCY. We're gonna set new standards. I feel it. I can legitimately *feel* it.

CAROLINE. Fuck yes Lucy!!! I feel it too!!!

CAROLINE LEAVES ANOTHER MESSAGE

(**CAROLINE** *and* **JESS** *wait to be picked up.* **JESS** *is on her phone.*)

CAROLINE. That went awesome.

JESS. Yeah

CAROLINE. So. So. Awesome.

JESS. For sure.

CAROLINE. Thanks for telling me to run for Dance Captain.

JESS. Sure.

CAROLINE. I love choreo – I honestly think I like it just as much as performing.

JESS. No prob.

CAROLINE. Are you okay?

JESS. Yeah?

CAROLINE. Thank god you came up with the cocoa powder idea! That was like. A total coup.

JESS. Yep

CAROLINE. A minute ago you seemed pumped?

JESS. I am pumped.

CAROLINE. So then why are you being weird?

JESS. What am I doing that's weird?

CAROLINE. You're like. Not looking at me.

JESS. (*Looking at her.*) Happy?

CAROLINE. ...Yeah.

JESS. See you tomorrow.

(**JESS** *exits.* **CAROLINE** *pulls out her phone.*)

CAROLINE. Hi. It's me. Um. I'm just calling because.

Um.

Did I do something?

If I did something

I just wanna know if I did something.

Because if you tell me what I did. Then I can fix it. But if you won't. If you won't call me back and tell me what I did then I then I can't fix it. And. That isn't fair. That isn't fair. If there's a problem and you don't tell someone, then they can't fix it and that's not /

MINDY. Hey Caroline!

CAROLINE. *(Snapping.)* I'm on the phone!

MINDY. Oh. Sorry.

>   *(**CAROLINE** gets up and runs off. **MINDY** yells after her.)*

Sorry Caroline!

....Sorry.

>   *(Blackout.)*

FACES PART 3

> (**THE TEAM** *is lined up downstage.* **LIZ** *is in the audience. Sorta talks to the group, sorta talks to the flag.*)

LIZ. Wonder!

> (**THE TEAM** *makes a face of wonder.*)

Shame!

> (**THE TEAM** *makes a face of shame.*)

Tall!

> (**THE TEAM** *tries to make a face that seems tall.*)

Secretive!

> (**THE TEAM** *tries to look secretive.*)

You're tall! But it's a secret!

> (**THE TEAM** *tries to look tall but in a secret way.*)

Pickled

LUCY. These don't make sense.

JESS. It's Liz's day Lucy.

LUCY. If we're gonna do face rehearsal it should make sense.

CAROLINE. It's just one day Lucy.

MAYA. I kind of agree with Lucy I mean if you think about it these feelings don't really make sense /

LIZ. *(To her flag.)* A feeling doesn't have to make sense for it to be true.

JESS. ...

...

Keep going Liz.

It's your day.

LIZ. Sunburnt!

(Blackout.)

LIZ'S LAST NIGHT AT THE CLUB

(**LIZ** *does a vicious but also incredible, gyrating, physical, hip-hop-but-not-hip-hop...her own dance to some rager of a song.* * *Her flag holds its own. It's her last night at the club – before she melts. Or maybe she's just unwinding after a tense rehearsal.*)

(*Blackout.*)

---

* A license to produce *The Winter Guard Play* does not include a performance license for any third-party or copyrighted music. Licensees should create an original composition or use music in the public domain. For further information, please see the Music and Third-Party Materials Use Note on page iii

WEEK 7: THE REHEARSAL HALL IS COLD

*(**LUCY** and **MAYA** have just arrived. Taking off jackets.)*

MAYA. It's completely crazy how cold it is in here.

LUCY. Yep

MAYA. It's nippy. It's so nippy.

LUCY. Why do you say things like nippy?

MAYA. My dad says nippy. He says, "Get in the car girls. It's nippy!"

LUCY. *(Not mean just fact.)* Wow. Our dads would not hang out.

MAYA. Why is the school so cold on weekends??

LUCY. Here's MY question, why does the school never turn on the heat when we ALWAYS rehearse the Saturday before States?!?!

MAYA. Sometimes it's like no one knows we exist

LUCY. They're gonna know after we CRUSH it next week.

MAYA. I feel really chilly. I feel like I need to take a soak.

LUCY. I love taking soaks. It's like literally all that I do at home.

MAYA. Really?

LUCY. Yeah. I take like six baths a week.

MAYA. Wow.

LUCY. Now that it's just me and my dad it's like there's nothing else to do but watch *American Ninja Warrior* and take baths you know?

MAYA. Oh my god. That makes me so sad.

LUCY. I'm not saying it in a sad way, I'm just saying it in a fact way.

MAYA. My hands are so dry.

LUCY. Okay?

MAYA. It's taken me like a week to get the fake blood off.

LUCY. It's just chocolate?

MAYA. Yeah but it's still like under my fingernails. I can't get it out I keep chewing on them and it's still there.

LUCY. Okay...

MAYA. I keep biting my cuticles and making myself actually bleed.

LUCY. Well. Stop?

MAYA. I can't stop I can't get the stupid stuff off my hands!

LUCY. It'll come off eventually...

MAYA. This year is so much harder.

LUCY. Well I mean last year we did some weird stuff

MAYA. But not blood.

LUCY. Last year we had the insulin prologue?

MAYA. It wasn't blood and drowning and I'm like having nightmares where I'm underwater just like drowning and drowning and no one cares!

LUCY. Are you /

MAYA. I can't even do my homework like yesterday I didn't do my homework I just stayed up all night reading stuff on the internet.

LUCY. Maya

MAYA. And then on top of that my fingers are actually bleeding because I can't stop freaking chewing on them.

LUCY. Sit down.

MAYA. I just. I just. I just I just I just.

LUCY. Or lay down.

(**MAYA** *lays down.*)

MAYA. Sorry.

LUCY. Why are you freaking out?

MAYA. Where are the seniors?

LUCY. Getting the tarp.

MAYA. Please don't say anything.

LUCY. Okay.

MAYA. Jess already hates me.

(*Beat.*)

I just. I just. I just don't know. I don't feel okay. I don't feel okay. Do you ever not feel okay?

LUCY. Regularly.

(*Beat.*)

MAYA. I think I'm depressed

LUCY. Really?

MAYA. I don't know. All the blood. And the dying. It's sadder than I thought it would be.

LUCY. You mean the theme?

MAYA. Yeah. The theme makes me very sad.

LUCY. (*Authentically confused.*) But the choreo looks good?

MAYA. No like

The actual global warming part.

MAYA. It's like

I forget about it.

And I just want us to win.

And then I remember

And then it feels like stupid to even be excited about going to college or like my life or my future.

And then it just feels like

Who cares about winning you know?

LUCY. I'm obsessed with winning so…I don't really know.

MAYA. Yeah.

(Beat.)

LUCY. *(Trying to reach out but not very good at it.)* If it makes you feel any better I've been feeling very volatile lately

MAYA. *(You're always volatile?)* …Really?

LUCY. Yeah! Like I'm doing random mean things.

MAYA. Like what?

LUCY. Like. I didn't vote for Caroline for Dance Captain.

MAYA. What! Why?

LUCY. I don't know

MAYA. Did you want to be Dance Captain?

LUCY. Yeah in the moment I guess

MAYA. But you don't enjoy choreo?

LUCY. I know.

MAYA. Plus you like Caroline don't you?

LUCY. It's not about that. Something just came over me.

MAYA. And you and Liz are already like the stars of the team. You don't need to be Dance Captain.

LUCY. Yeah and you retook the SATs when you lost what, twenty points on verbal?

MAYA. Ten. But yeah.

LUCY. It's just never enough you know? We all always want more. I guess that's like...why the Earth is dying.

MAYA. I guess so.

(*Finding her resolve.*) You're right. We have one week left. I can do this.

Flectere si nequeo superos, Acheronta movebo.

LUCY. I'm failing Latin Maya.

MAYA. If I cannot bend the will of Heaven, I shall move Hell.

(**ZOE** *and* **LIZ** *enter.*)

ZOE. It was the climax of the show!! Like the peak. The absolute peak. Like the summit. The summit of the play.

MAYA. Hey guys!

ZOE. It's the most important song. The most important /

MAYA. Hello guys!

ZOE. Oh yo!! Sorry didn't see ya I'm like too consumed by RAGE.

LUCY. What are you talking about?

ZOE. The MUSICAL. It was criminal.

MAYA. Ohhh yes. I heard about this.

ZOE. It should be on like the NEWS or something. It was so bad.

LUCY. Rob Peters?

ZOE. Yes. YES. And he just. He CRACKED. Like not a little bit. Like a lot a bit. And it wouldn't stop. It was like an actual avalanche. It was so painful to the ears.

MAYA. Wow.

LUCY. I heard they took the mic out?

ZOE. Oh yeah they took it out alright. But it didn't help. He was so loud and SO bad.

MAYA. He's tall but not talented.

LUCY. He can't sing.

MAYA. All that length, but no gift.

LIZ. *(To her flag.)* Not like you.

ZOE. It was INSANE.

MAYA. He should stop doing musicals.

LUCY. They should stop casting him!!

ZOE. This has happened before?!??!?!

LIZ. *(To her flag, spitefully.) Little Shop.*

MAYA. *(She's thought about this a lot.)* It's just 'cause he's tall. There's no other guy in our grade who's that tall.

ZOE. But he's BAD!!!!

LUCY. The worst production of *Little Shop* in human history.

MAYA. I wish that plant had eaten him earlier.

ZOE. My head is SPINNING right now.

MAYA. Someone really should tell him.

LUCY. Yeah like who?? How do you say to someone "you're not talented"?

MAYA. Didn't Rachel Sherman do that? Our freshman year?

ZOE. Seriously?????

MAYA. It was before I was on the team...but that's true right Lucy?

LUCY. Rachel was cutthroat.

ZOE. What did she do?

LUCY. She told this girl who like kept messing up and dropping flags and like tripping over things and stuff. She told her she could get off the team or be water girl.

MAYA. I remember I was in her calc class and she came in one day and her face was all puffy like she'd been crying for days. And at first I thought she was just crying because she was very bad at calculus but it was actually because she was made water girl.

ZOE. Wow

MAYA. Very sad.

LUCY. Rachel was awesome though.

ZOE. Sounds like a scary chick

MAYA. She started freestyle right?

LUCY. Yes ALWAYS to "Toxic."

MAYA. We haven't done that in a very long time.

ZOE. What's freestyle?

LUCY. Just like playing music and dancing around

ZOE. What??? Let's do it!!!

LUCY. Uh...

MAYA. It is objectively fun...

ZOE. It's just like playing music and doing whatever we want?

MAYA. Correct

ZOE. LET'S DO IT.

MAYA. Okay!!

(**MAYA** *plugs in her phone. Some Top 40 song plays.*)

(*It's really loud.* **ZOE** *lets loose. Runs around like a gazelle hopped up on molly. Beautiful but also very crazy to watch.*)

(**LIZ** *immediately grabs her flag and starts to dance with it enthusiastically.* **MAYA** *and* **LUCY** *dance together. Awkward but nice.* **CAROLINE** *enters. On her phone. Sees the dancing. Hangs up. Dances towards them.* **JESS** *enters. Joins.* **MINDY** *enters. Wants to die. Walks over to* **LIZ**, *and sways awkwardly.*)

(*Suddenly the music changes to violent, rageful party music.* **THE TEAM** *suddenly moves in unison in a riotous, cathartic, demon-purging dance.*)

(*Then the music cuts out.*)

(*All at once they fall down on top of each other. Are they dead?*)

(*Suddenly, they begin to chant in a whisper.*)

THE TEAM. *(Unison.)* Look what you did to me, look what you did to me, look what you did to me. Look what you did to me. Look what you did to me.

---

* A license to produce *The Winter Guard Play* does not include a performance license for any third-party or copyrighted music. Licensees should create an original composition or use music in the public domain. For further information, please see the Music and Third-Party Materials Use Note on page iii.

FLASHBACK: SOPHOMORE YEAR!

(**JESS** and **CAROLINE** *peek their heads out of the pile. They are all of a sudden, fifteen. They are at a sleepover.*)

(*Whispered.*)

JESS. Today was amazing.

CAROLINE. So. So. Amazing.

JESS. They are so good.

CAROLINE. The seniors?

JESS. Oh my god they're amazing.

CAROLINE. Like so amazing.

JESS. Rachel!

CAROLINE. Literally an ICON

JESS. And Coach!

CAROLINE. She is so scary.

JESS. She's incredible.

CAROLINE. Did you hear she went to Nationals when she was in high school?

JESS. Caroline she WON Nationals when she was in high school.

CAROLINE. I hope she likes me.

JESS. I can't wait for my parents to see the show.

CAROLINE. Your mom is going to love it.

JESS. She's gonna go INSANE

CAROLINE. Oh my god your mom is gonna be like with her iPad like filming the whole thing.

JESS. *(Less whispered.)* Shut up!!!

CAROLINE. Your mom brings her iPad everywhere.

JESS. Shut up!!!

CAROLINE. Like is she scared someone's gonna steal it?!

JESS. *(Not whispered.)* I hate you!!!

CAROLINE. Wait shhhhh!!

>   *(They giggle.)*

JESS. How late is it??

CAROLINE. Almost two!

JESS. Wow. So late.

You should sleep over every Friday after practice.

CAROLINE. Can we do arm tickles?

JESS. Fineeee

>   **(JESS** *and* **CAROLINE** *hold each other's forearms face up and tickle them.)*

We're gonna be unreal seniors.

CAROLINE. Oh my god. That's SO cool to think about.

JESS. Everyone will be like obsessed with us.

CAROLINE. Our senior year is gonna be EPIC.

JESS. It's gonna be so good. It's gonna be so so good.

>   *(Beat. The two get cozy. Drifting into sleep.)*

I love Winter Guard so much.

I love it so much that sometimes it like literally kinda hurts.

Like it makes my chest feel tight, but not 'cause I'm anxious.

It's not like my chest is tight in a scared way.

It's like when I do Winter Guard, and when it's just going really really well.

It's like my heart gets really big and it feels like it's filling up my arms and all my fingers and my toes and I'm like this flag heart monster and my chest gets tight 'cause I don't know if my body is built to hold this much.

It's just so big.

CAROLINE. Yeah like you could explode.

JESS. Totally.

CAROLINE. But in a good way. In a really good way.

> *(They drift to sleep. Lights change.* **CAROLINE** *stands.)*

And that would be the final image.

JESS. *(From the body pile.)* Wait before everyone gets up. Can you take a picture with your phone? So we can see?

CAROLINE. Yes yes!

ZOE. I cannot believe it's tomorrow!!!

MINDY. I feel sick.

ZOE. Twenty-four HOURS!!!

CAROLINE. Wait, lemme find my phone.

MINDY. I feel like I'm gonna throw up.

JESS. Zoe can your brother look at the audio?

MINDY. Someone is laying on me.

ZOE. Is it me?

JESS. I wanna be sure that glitch with the announcer doesn't happen again.

LUCY. Let's do it again and film it.

CAROLINE. It's normally in my pencil case hold on /

MINDY. Someone is on top of me!

CAROLINE. Just one sec Mindy

MAYA. Does anyone have a tripod with them?

MINDY. I CAN'T FEEL MY HANDS

JESS. Fine! Everyone just stand up!

> (**THE TEAM** *stands up.* **MINDY** *crouches with her head between her legs, as if having a panic attack.*)

CAROLINE. What's wrong?

MINDY. It's not right.

CAROLINE. Mindy do you need to /

MINDY. The ending. The ending it's not right.

JESS. Okay. What don't you like?

MINDY. Is that.

Is that…

Is that what you all want to say?

Is that like what you want to say to our parents and everyone?

We're all gonna die?

You think we're all gonna die??

LIZ. *(To her flag.)* We are all gonna die.

JESS. What Liz?

MAYA. She said we are all going to die. Which is correct.

MINDY. But but but

Not tomorrow

Not soon

And it's

And it's our parents fault??

You want to tell them all

Right to their

Right to their faces

That it's all their fault?

JESS. Mindy that's not what we're trying to /

LUCY. Yeah! That is what we're saying!

CAROLINE. Wait Lucy /

LUCY. I don't care!

JESS. Okay Lucy /

LUCY. I don't care about making our parents feel bad!

I don't care!

They should feel bad

They should feel bad

It's like who gives a fuck what college I get into

I ethically shouldn't procreate.

Do you guys get that?

We ethically shouldn't have children?

Because they won't be able to go outside

Do you get how sad that is???

Our parents screwed us.

MINDY. Well I don't feel that way!

I... I don't feel that way!

I love my parents!

I love my parents and I love my grandparents

MINDY. And and and

I don't want to invite them to a show just to

Just to

Just to say

Fuck you!

That's not what I want to do.

LUCY. GLOBAL WARMING WAS YOUR IDEA

MINDY. WELL I WISH I HAD NEVER SAID IT

LUCY. TOO LATE! YOU DID!

CAROLINE. LUCY stop!!

MAYA. Mindy. This is bigger than us.

MINDY. I don't want the dance

I don't want the dance to end with all of us dead.

I don't... I don't... If we end all of us dead

I'm dropping out.

I will not invite my mom

To watch me die

LUCY. Mindy. It's acting. It's pretend.

CAROLINE. Guys /

MAYA. How else Mindy? How else do we let them know? What's gonna happen??? Do you want to grow up Mindy?? Do you want to have children and and go for walks and go sledding?? This isn't about making people feel GOOD Mindy. Do you get that???

MINDY. I don't like thinking there is no hope

MAYA. THERE IS NO HOPE.

MINDY. I don't think that – that's not how I think!

MAYA. Well then how do you think we should end it??

MINDY. I don't know I don't know I don't know

LUCY. Ohhhh great. So you don't have an alternate plan.

MAYA. What about the NRDC MINDY!!?!? Do you hate the NRDC???!

MINDY. I can't remember what those letters stand FOR!!! And my parents don't even HAVE enough money to donate to the NRDC and then they'll be MAD at me for embarrassing them in front of the other parents AND THEN SAYING FUCK YOU AND DYING!!!!

       (Beat.)

CAROLINE. Okay. Maybe we can change the ending.

JESS. No we can't. It's tomorrow.

CAROLINE. Jess, Mindy is really upset

MAYA. This is why I was worried about not having a coach.

JESS. SHUT UP MAYA.

CAROLINE. Jess!!

JESS. Fine. Fine. Call Coach.

MAYA. I didn't mean /

JESS. No. It's fine. Let's call Coach. Why don't you call her Caroline?

CAROLINE. What? No!

JESS. It'll be better coming from you.

CAROLINE. I'm not gonna call her.

JESS. Why not?

CAROLINE. I don't know because /

JESS. Or I'll call her! Caroline can I borrow your phone?

CAROLINE. What?

JESS. Where's your phone?

CAROLINE. What?

JESS. Where's your phone give me your phone I'm gonna call coach

CAROLINE. No.

JESS. Where's your phone Caroline??

CAROLINE. I'm not telling you!!

LUCY. Guys /

(**JESS** *is going through Caroline's bag.*)

CAROLINE. Stop it! Stop going through my stuff!

LUCY. What is happening??

CAROLINE. This isn't fair you've been so mad at me all year for no reason

JESS. No reason???

MAYA. What's going on??

JESS. Here it is /

CAROLINE. Jess wait please don't look at my /

JESS. Why not??

CAROLINE. Because it's not what it /

JESS. I KNEW IT!

I KNEW YOU WERE CALLING HER.

CAROLINE. It doesn't have anything to do with you!

JESS. Doesn't have anything to do with me???

CAROLINE. Just because I call Coach /

JESS. She humiliated me Caroline! In front of everyone!

CAROLINE. I know I know I was just asking her for help I was just asking her for –

JESS. You would throw anyone under the bus for a "good job Caroline."

CAROLINE. Shut up.

JESS. *(Impersonating Coach.)* "Nice form Caroline."

CAROLINE. You're an asshole.

JESS. "Good catch Caroline."

CAROLINE. IT'S NOT MY FAULT I'M BETTER AT WINTER GUARD THAN YOU!

JESS. ...

CAROLINE. Jess. Wait I didn't mean that I /

MAYA. Guys guys, guys!!

Mindy's gone.

(Blackout.)

MINDY PRAYS ONE MORE TIME

MINDY. Hi God. It's me. Mindy.

I'm sorry.

I feel like you're probably mad at me.

You didn't make me a whole new person.

And so. That must mean. You thought that was a bad thing to ask for. Sorry

...

I feel like. When I got better.

I thought things would be different.

Or like. I thought I would be wiser? I mean everyone tells you when you go through something like that, you get wiser.

But I don't feel wiser. I don't even feel older.

I feel like I'm still in seventh grade and while I was getting better...everyone grew up without me.

I feel really behind.

Am I just gonna be behind forever? And care about things no one cares about? I want to do the things that everyone else does and feel the things that everyone else feels.

Maybe I'm being a baby about the theme.

I can be angry – I can say the f word!

...But I can't do the show that way.

I can't do that ending. My mom can't see that ending.

And I don't like what it says. I don't like that.

It's like...if there's no hope...why did I get better?

...

If I do that ending…I don't think I'll ever be able to do Winter Guard again.

I just think it'll always feel different.

…

Will you give me a sign? I know that's a lot to ask but I'd really like a sign to tell me what to do. I don't need to be a whole new person. I just want to be the sort of person who knows what to do.

WEEK 8: STATES

> (**MAYA, LIZ, LUCY** *and* **ZOE** *sit in a circle.*
> **JESS** *sits apart. Everyone is on their phones.*
> *Long silence.* **CAROLINE** *enters.)*

CAROLINE. Hey. Can we huddle?

JESS. Did you sign us in?

CAROLINE. There's a problem.

JESS. Whatever.

MAYA. *(Raises hand.)* Mindy hasn't come.

CAROLINE. Well then. Two problems. Can someone call
  Mindy?

ZOE. Because everyone yelled at herrrrr

LUCY. None of us have her number.

ZOE. I could DM her?

CAROLINE. Do that.

LUCY. What's the problem?

CAROLINE. Can everyone please just huddle up??

JESS. Why??

ZOE. Shoot she doesn't even have Instagram.

CAROLINE. Because I don't want the whole hall to hear us!

JESS. Fine.

> *(Everyone huddles.)*

CAROLINE. They won't let us perform without a coach.

JESS. What??

CAROLINE. They said we need an adult to sign us in.

JESS. Fuck.

MAYA. I KNEW this would happen

CAROLINE. What should we do?

JESS. Shit. Shit.

CAROLINE. I don't think we can compete...

ZOE. Noooooooo!!

LUCY. Well unless Mindy shows we can't even do it. There'll be all these flags that are never picked up.

MAYA. Perhaps this is the end

ZOE. GUYS NOOOOO we gotta!!!

JESS. Are there any other teachers here?

LUCY. No. No one cares about Winter Guard.

MAYA. I invited Mrs. Plutzker.

JESS. Did she come??

MAYA. No, she had a bat mitzvah.

ZOE. Waitttttt. Does anyone have a parent here?

JESS. YES... We need a mom. They don't know what Coach looks like.

CAROLINE. Right! They just have her name!

LUCY. Whose mom is here?

MAYA. Jess?

JESS. Everyone knows my mom, she's like the fucking mayor.

ZOE. My brother's here.

LUCY. My dad's here...

MAYA. My parents are here. But they won't lie. They wouldn't wanna get disbarred.

CAROLINE. Shit.

MINDY. What's going on?

>(**MINDY** *has entered.*)

ZOE. MINDY!!! YOU'RE ALIVE!

CAROLINE. They won't let us sign in without a coach.

JESS. We're doomed.

LUCY. No come on, if Mindy is here we can do it.

MINDY. What's going on?

CAROLINE. We need an adult who can sign us in.

MINDY. An adult?

ZOE. Let's just go in the stands walk around, find a random adult. Play the sympathy card.

MINDY. I'm confused.

CAROLINE. We need a woman who can pretend to be Coach.

ZOE. If we just go around and cry someone will pretend to be Coach.

JESS. If we go around and cry people will notice and then we'll get caught.

ZOE. ...Shoot.

JESS. We're fucked.

LUCY. Guys come on there has to be a way to do this.

MAYA. I think we should back out.

MINDY. *(Quietly.)* No.

CAROLINE. I'm sorry guys I'm so /

LIZ. Mindy said something.

ZOE. What Mindy?

MINDY. We don't have to back out. I know what to do. My mom can do it.

CAROLINE. She'd pretend to be Coach?

MINDY. Yes.

JESS. She would do that?

MINDY. She knows how important this is to me.

ZOE. HALLELUJAAAAAHHH

LUCY. Mindy. YES.

ZOE. BLESS YOU MINDY!!!

MINDY. But not with the ending like this.

CAROLINE. Okay okay. Let's just get the Coach stuff cleared up and then we can figure it out /

MINDY. I'm not asking my mom, until we change the ending.

CAROLINE. Mindy we don't have that much time to sign in.

MINDY. I won't do it.

CAROLINE. Please Mindy can you just /

MINDY. No.

JESS. Can you just get over it.

MINDY. No.

JESS. Why??

MINDY. Because. That's how I fucking feel.

> *(Woah.)*

CAROLINE. Okay.

Does anyone have any ideas?

MAYA. Um. What if we simply pass out and uhhhh don't die?

LUCY. How would they know the difference?

MAYA. ...We sit up and say, "we lived!"

(Woof.)

JESS. Any other ideas?

CAROLINE. We just cut the blood all together?

ZOE. Noo!!!!!

JESS. It took us the whole season to figure out the blood
we can't cut it.

ZOE. The blood is extraordinary it's so so essential.

JESS. Plus we'd have to change too much. We're on in less
than an hour.

CAROLINE. Mindy it just might not be possible

MINDY. My mom's waiting for me in the car. I can tell her
I wanna go home.

MAYA. No no!! Do not do that!!

ZOE. We should have done a different themeeeee. UGH.

CAROLINE. Mindy, please.

ZOE. We had so many other ideassss

LUCY. No. Mindy. Wait.

We can change the ending.

JESS. What?

CAROLINE. Lucy. What are you talking about?

MAYA. Lucy. Are you joshing?

LUCY. No. We can change the ending. Does everyone
remember Zoe's child labor presentation?

(Blackout.)

BEFORE THE LAST EARTH DAY

*(***CAROLINE*** and **JESS** *crouch downstage as*
THE TEAM *sets up behind them.)*

CAROLINE. …

> …

> Do you think we're gonna pull this off?

JESS. I don't know.

CAROLINE. Yeah.

> …

> I'm sorry for calling Coach.

JESS. …

CAROLINE. I hate her.

JESS. No you don't.

CAROLINE. I do. It's just. For a long time. Hearing good
job from Coach seemed like. The whole point of. I don't
know.

JESS. Being alive?

CAROLINE. Yeah.

JESS. Me too.

CAROLINE. But I think it's amazing you yelled at her.
I think it's amazing you yelled back.

JESS. …Thanks.

CAROLINE. And I'm glad she quit.

JESS. No you aren't.

CAROLINE. Yes I am. I'm really glad we did this last year
together.

JESS. …

You know. You are better at Winter Guard than me.

CAROLINE. No I'm /

JESS. No you are. You really are.

When you caught my flag last year. I was so relieved. And I was so embarrassed.

CAROLINE. Yeah.

JESS. It's just been a hard time. For me.

CAROLINE. *(Nodding.)* Yeah. Me too.

ANNOUNCER. Performing their program, "The Last Earth Day," WGI Sports is proud to present Mechanicsfield High School.

(Same configuration as start of play. **LIZ** *does an incredible solo throughout the start.)*

LUCY. My Earth.

JESS. My planet.

MAYA. My oceans.

CAROLINE. My mountains.

MINDY. My sky.

MAYA. My air.

LIZ. Clear.

JESS. Blue.

ZOE. Green.

MAYA. Beautiful.

CAROLINE. Beautiful.

LIZ. Beautiful.

LUCY. Sinking.

JESS. My city.

LUCY. Sinking.

CAROLINE. My town.

LUCY. Drowning.

MAYA. My forest.

LUCY. Burning.

CAROLINE. My creatures.

LUCY. Dying.

MINDY. Floods.

MAYA. Flooding me.

LIZ. Flooding you

CAROLINE. My Earth.

JESS. My Earth.

LIZ. My Earth.

THE TEAM. *(Unison.)* Look what you /

    (Spotlight on **LIZ.***)*

LIZ TALKS TO HER FLAG

LIZ. I know you're nervous.

I'm nervous too.

But look.

We've done this before.

We're so ready.

We've done this what?

A thousand times.

I'm going to catch you.

Don't worry.

Don't be scared.

Today is your day.

And if something happened to me.

If I fell. Or if I got sick. Or if I just messed up.

That happens you know.

I could mess up.

If any of that happens.

They would catch you.

I know I don't let you talk to them much.

But it's only because they all have so many friends.

And I just have you.

It's selfish.

I'm sorry.

You would feel safer probably

If I'd let you talk to them.

I messed up.

Look I avoid them

'Cause I don't know

I like hanging out with you more.

But they are good.

They are really good.

I can tell.

And look.

Even though

They don't know me that well

And even though

I don't think we'll be friends when the season ends

Even though we might not see them once we graduate

Even though all of them think I'm weird.

I love them.

I think I'm gonna love them until I'm dead.

I'm gonna love them forever.

And the people you love

Take care of the other things you love.

And I love you.

So don't worry.

Even if I died on the floor

Even if I drop dead right now

They'd catch you.

 (Lights up.)

(Music. **THE TEAM** snaps into the riotous, cathartic, demon-purging unison dance on page 74.)*

(Their mouths drip with blood.)

(Flags and ribbons are splayed across the stage.)

(The combination is almost done.)

(The music cuts out.)

(All at once they fall down on top of each other. We've seen this body pile before.)

(Are they dead?)

*(And then **LUCY** sits up. She reaches over and puts her hand on **MINDY**'s back. She rubs her back. Very maternal. And then she rips the back of **MINDY**'s shirt. And underneath there are wings. **MINDY** sits up. She feels her wings. She reaches over to **ZOE**'s back. Rips her shirt. There are wings. **ZOE** does this to **JESS**. And so on and so on.)*

(Until they are all in a line. Surrounding the earth tarp. The Earth on the tarp begins to slowly bleed.)

THE TEAM. *(Chanting.)* I'm free

    I'm free

    I'm free

---

* A license to produce *The Winter Guard Play* does not include a performance license for any third-party or copyrighted music. Licensees should create an original composition or use music in the public domain. For further information, please see the Music and Third-Party Materials Use Note on page iii.

I'm free

I'm FREE

I'm FREE

I'm FREE

I'm FREE

I'm FREE

FREE

FREE

FREE

FREEEEEEEEE!!!!!!

> (**MINDY** *steps forward.*)

MINDY. Nothing is free.

> (**MINDY** *takes off her wings. They are made out of towels? She begins to wipe the blood off the Earth. One by one* **THE TEAM** *joins her. They take off their wings. They wipe the blood off the Earth.*)
>
> (**LIZ** *stands up. Picks up her flag.*)
>
> (*Throws it with great force.*)
>
> (*And just before she catches it.*)
>
> (*Lights out.*)

End of Play

APPENDIX

The current script of *The Winter Guard Play* is written for productions that wish to use fake blood onstage. If productions would like opt out of using fake blood, they can implement the following dialogue changes:

PAGE 60:

JESS. Cocoa power instead of corn syrup

CAROLINE. Huge difference. We tested it. Huge, huge difference.

> *Changes to*

JESS. We have a new plan for the blood I'll go over it today.

CAROLINE. It's really cool guys.

JESS. Turns out all fake blood is sticky but this is gonna be better.

PAGE 62:

CAROLINE. Thank god you came up with the cocoa powder idea! That was like. A total coup.

> *Changes to*

CAROLINE. I think the new idea for the blood is gonna be awesome.

PAGE 68:

LUCY. It's just chocolate?

> *Changes to*

LUCY. Well we're not using it anymore so /